I0520312

Married, Divorced, Remarried

by Dr. Moses Oluwole

Copyright © 2020
All Rights Reserved
ISBN: 978-1-7356552-2-2

INTRODUCTION

When James Rosenberg saw his wife's shocked expression the day he walked out of Petra's door, he knew he was in trouble— the exemplary Christian family man is faced with a nightmarish situation after he cheated on his wife with the stunning Petra Gonzalez. He doesn't only risk losing the respect of all the whole church, his wife Carla wants a divorce...

With support from his best friend Pastor Elias Potter, and repentant partner in crime Petra Gonzalez, James is ready to fight for his wife's love once more and convince her he is truly sorry...

The Christian couple face a turbulent week full of extraordinary events— fatal accidents, heart attacks, and near-death experiences. But will the adrenaline and blood-thumping experiences have any effect on the icy cold resolve of Carla Rosenberg, or James has truly lost his wife and the mother of his six-month old baby forever?

Table of Contents

CHAPTER ONE

Pressed against the cold, wet wall, he felt the blade pierce his tummy without warning, shocking him and sending him towards the brink of unconsciousness. He gaped, his watery eyes staring up at his perpetrator as his mouth hung open, unable to produce a sound. As the blade of the knife twisted inside him, the pain he thought was the worst possible only got worse... He felt his vision darkening and blurring, and wondered if he was actually dying.

"Jesus-Jesus!" James was stuttering... He was having trouble swallowing, and then he was having trouble even breathing. His limbs were growing weaker by the second, and he felt himself sliding down the wall.

Was this how it felt to die?

The man who stood above him in the dark alley was laughing—a cynical, mocking laugh that did not make things any better.

"Jesus? That's all you can say? What the hell?" He laughed.

The big man grabbed his neck, his rough fingers feeling like fresh unused sandpaper around his throat. With a quick jerking motion, he withdrew his knife, letting go of James.

As he fell facedown to the wet alley floor, he lost consciousness before he made impact.

Ten days earlier…

James watched with a grim expression on his face. Standing at the base of the stairs, he could do nothing as Carla dragged her suitcase towards the door angrily. At the door, she turned to glare at him.

"God will punish you, James!"

Her stinging words pierced him like a mogul's arrow, and he retorted, "Why would he? Why would he when you are acting like a hypocrite?"

She let go of the suitcase's handle, allowing it to hit the tiled floor in a loud slap.

"What did you say?" Fury burned in her moist eyes. "James, what did you just say to me?"

He struggled with himself. Her tears were always a weakness he couldn't overcome, but the anger and pride bubbling in him pushed aside his sentiments, "Why are you acting so dramatic as if I killed someone? I said I was sorry but—"

"Sorry?! Look at you! Do you *look* sorry? You cheat on me when you have a six-month old baby, and you stand there telling me you said sorry?"

"Going to mum won't help; let's talk about this—"

"I'm done talking; I need some space. Don't call me, and don't come there!" She jabbed a finger at him.

"What happened to forgiveness, Carla? Isn't that what you're supposed to do? Forgive?"

She blinked, and more tears ran down her cheeks, "You are such a snake,"

"Carla, you're going too far," he felt his chest tighten.

"Too far? Did you think how far you were going when you were—'

"Enough of that! It's not like you haven't done anything wrong before!" he lashed out angrily, seeing the shock on her face, "What did I do when you kissed Todd? Did I pack my bags and go to my mother?!"

Immediately the words rumbled out, he knew they shouldn't have. She will definitely know that he was still angry about that incidence. Her college ex had bumped into her at the mall and had kissed her on impulse, unaware she had been married. *How?* He had been there, and he had seen it. It wasn't supposed to be a big deal... but it had never been right with him. Now that he had used that year-old excuse in such a bad time, he wondered what Carla would do.

She swallowed, deep blue eyes staring back at him, but this time, with no grief. They were ice cold. She brushed a hand through her long blonde hair, sniffing involuntarily.

"I want a divorce," the words came out.

He heard her alright, but it took another moment before it sank in. When it did, he realized he was struck speechless. Was that how far it had gone? Divorce?

He said nothing, he just stood there staring back at her.

"And I will keep Josh; a baby needs his mother," she said with finality and walked back to the front door. She picked up her suitcase again and walked out, closing the door behind her.

Still frozen on the stairs, James suddenly felt a nagging headache. He placed a hand over his forehead and winced at how cold his own hand was.

His phone rang, startling him for a second. He reached out into his back jeans pocket and took it out. Staring at the screen, he couldn't believe his eyes.

It was Petra. Hours after Carla had spotted him coming out of Petra's front door, she was calling him. With a sigh, he answered it.

"Hello,"

"Hey, how are you?"

"Is that what you can ask?"

"I'm just worried. How's Carla?"

"She's gone."

"What do you mean gone?" Petra sounded alarmed.

"She asked for a divorce,"

There was silence at the other side now.

"Hello?" He wondered if she had hung up.

"Umm—I'm sorry James, you know I never wanted—"

"Look, this was more than just a mistake, this is a disaster. Me—you, it was all wrong. I know I've missed my wife ever since the baby came into the picture, but it was not—"

"James, I love you," her voice was meek.

How could she say that when his world was crumbling?

"Are you crazy?" He felt renewed rage boiling in him.

"Please don't do that," Petra was beginning to sob, "Please…"

"My wife just left me, and you have the guts to say you love me!" He barked, "What kind of monster are you? Did you pray that we would get caught?!"

"Why would I do that? I never wanted this to happen," Her crying was getting louder.

Somehow he didn't feel any sympathy for her. All he felt was anger.

"Where did you think we were going with this? You think I was going to leave my wife for you?"

She said nothing, but her crying grew louder.

Shaking his head, James cut the connection and started to hit another set of numbers quickly. There was only one person he could speak to now; his best friend Pastor Elias Potter.

Carla pulled into the driveway, and then saw Hannah Madsen coming out her front door. Her mother looked worried.

She had stopped crying earlier, but as she looked at the sad face of her mother, she felt the grief starting to gnaw at her all over again. What happened to James? They were such a perfect Christian couple.

By the time the engine's fire died down, Hannah was standing by the driver's door of her white Mini Cooper. As soon as Carla opened her door, she felt fresh tears pelting down her face.

"Oh darling!" Hannah shook her head, arms opening for her.

Carla fell into her mother's arms, shuddering as she started to weep afresh.

"He's such a monster, mum," she managed to say amidst the tears, "he's a monster,"

"Hush baby," Hannah stroked her hair, rocking her in her arms gently, "come let's go inside. Your son is awake."

She drew back, sniffing, "I asked for a divorce, mum."

Hannah looked like she was struck by thunder, "You *what*?"

"Mum, he cheated on me!" Carla scowled, "And then he had the guts to point a finger at *me*! I can't live with such a selfish—"

"Carla, this is all happening too fast, calm down. This is the time that God expects you to—"

"To what, mum? God expects me to what? To shut up and suffer?"

"No, darling," Hannah may have realized she wasn't going to listen to any sermon there, "let's go inside. I think Josh is crying. We can come back for your bags later."

Carla only nodded, somewhat angry her mother had not supported her verdict. Whatever the case, she was sure of her decision—and nothing was going to change it.

James listened as the phone rang for the seventh time without an answer. As soon as he heard the beep, he cut the connection and decided he would drive to Elias' house. He only hoped his wife wouldn't be around.

A minute later, he was heading back down the stairs when he heard the doorbell ring.

Who could have such awful timing?

Grunting, he answered as he approached, "Who is it?"

"Bad time?" Elias' familiar deep voice was a relief.

"Eli!" He yanked the door open quickly, and saw Elias gazing back with his usual ear-to-ear grin.

He had the build of an athlete, only he had ended his athletic dreams after joining the pastoral school after college. Naturally a hairy fellow, he kept a thick but neat brown beard that dovetailed with a thick moustache.

"You look like you've had a good beating, brother," Elias smiled, "what's the matter?"

James' smile of relief waned, and he opened the door wider, "Please come in, we need to talk."

As Elias entered the sitting room, he looked around, "Where's Carla? Still not back from her mum's?"

James turned around to face him, swallowing hard, "Eli, that's what I need to talk to you about,"

Elias looked confused, because his thick brows burrowed as he placed his familiar thick old Bible on the centre table. He sat in the couch and looked over at James, who was perched at the edge of the couch facing the hairy man.

"So, you have a problem with your wife staying at her mother's?" Elias linked his fingers under his chin.

"No," James shook his head, "I screwed up, Eli," he felt the tears of shame stinging his eyes.

Elias was clearly not comfortable seeing a fellow man close to tears, "Hey calm down and tell me what happened, brother,"

"I really, really screwed up…" James wiped his eyes with the back of his hand before looking over at the curious pastor, "I cheated on her."

He saw Elias gape. He stared back at James, unable to say a word.

"It's over for me now, isn't it?" James shook his head slowly, sniffing.

Elias seemed to have gained his composure—at least some of it, because he cleared his throat and shifted in his seat, "James, tell me *exactly* what happened. Take your time—and it's not over. Go on..."

"Eli," James looked him in the eye, "I just missed her—I didn't want to, but..."

"Who was it?" His question was intended to be a gentle one, but it sounded more like a hard one.

James swallowed, "Petra."

"*What*?" Uncharacteristically, Elias lost his composure, "Are you serious, James?!" he roared.

"Look, it just happened, and I have no idea how she came exactly at that time..."

Elias looked to have gotten over the initial shock. "Look, there are times when—"

"Eli, if you are going to say she will come back, she's not. She quoted Matthew 5:32 and then at the door, she asked for a divorce." James revealed.

"Listen," he leaned forward, "this may be a very dark time for the two of you, but it's not over until it's over. You *cannot* do this! Go and fight for her! You don't look like you *enjoyed* what happened. You regret it, so get out there and bring her back. Look, in 1 John 1:9, our Lord says that if we confess our sins, He is faithful and just to forgive our sins, and to cleanse us from all unrighteousness. She knows this, and her anger and hurt will pass. Don't give in to the divorce!"

"Right," James didn't sound convinced, "you should have seen her, Eli,"

"James, are you saying you won't go? You put your pride aside and get out!" Elias bellowed in the charismatic tone James had been accustomed to for fourteen years.

"I won't," James spoke coolly, "I wanted to speak to you as a friend, and also because she will talk to you about it, so I thought you should know that I am truly sorry."

"Look, please don't close me out. How did you and Petra do this? She's always admired you and Carla, so—"

"Not Carla, I've always known that they didn't get along."

"And yet you were still close to her," Elias shook his head.

"Are you going to judge me?"

"I wish I could," he sounded annoyed, "because your wife didn't like her, yet you—"

"I never did anything wrong—"

"Until now!" Elias yelled. "Do you have any idea what the church will think of you?"

"Are you going to say this in church?" James was shocked.

"Maybe not, but your wife could."

"She won't," James was sure, "she's not that kind of person. Look I will take your advice and go and see her. But not now when she still hates me. Please pray with me Eli, because I feel like my world is collapsing."

Elias nodded, "I will, but please brother, talk to God and ask for forgiveness for what you've done." Elias got up, picking up his Bible.

"Leaving?"

"Yeah, I need to see Petra too."

James blinked, "Oh,"

"Yes, what you're thinking is true. I'm going to talk to her about this, and please, stay away from her."

"After what happened, I am sure I can do that."

Petra was Hispanic, and she prided herself with picking all the good features from her Colombian mother and her American father. A great shapely body, smooth skin, and long brown hair complemented her 5'8 height. She would have been a model if she hadn't fallen in love with cooking early. At twenty-four, she was the proud co-owner of a Spanish restaurant in downtown Blue Fin.

As she looked at her bikini reflection in the mirror, she was not admiring herself at all. Her eyelids were swollen from crying and she could see the lines her mascara had drawn through the tears down her cheeks. She had fallen in love with the wrong man, it seemed. How cruel life could get! Men flung themselves at her, but she liked none. She had been drawn to the handsome and godly James Rosenberg—never mind he was married! Now, disaster had struck, and he was not at *her* side. They had had fun together in the last few weeks, and on the day they had lost control in her bungalow, Carla had appeared there.

She heard the unmistakable knock on her door and wondered who it was. She left the mirror in her bathroom and quickly grabbed the robe she had draped on her bed. As she put the robe on, she heard the knock again.

"I'm coming!" She called out, as she closed her bedroom door behind her and walked towards the door.

She unlocked the door, and froze. Standing and looking back calmly with a sympathetic expression was Pastor Elias Potter.

"My dear, what have you done?"

He knew.

"Pastor, I'm so, so sorry..."

CHAPTER TWO

She sat opposite the pastor, unable to say anything. He seemed to have taken it well. The Pastor Elias she knew would have been bellowing in rage at such an abominable act. Or would he?

"So, tell me what happened, Petra," he asked quietly, his big bible resting on his lap.

She shook her head, aware she was definitely going to cry if she uttered another word.

Elias furrowed his brows and leaned back in his seat, folding his arms, "Alright then, we will just wait until you are ready to tell us."

Why was he so cool about it? His coolness was even more unnerving. She decided she had to speak up, and get him out of this mood.

"Pastor," her hands went up to her eyes quickly cleaning the tears that were already running down, "I will stop coming to your church if that's what you want okay? I'll just—"

"That's not the problem, my little sister," his deep voice gentle but firm, "I want to help here. Do you think God enjoys watching you suffer like this?"

She nodded.

"Then you're wrong,"

"But I've sinned, haven't I?"

"Looks, God does not delight Himself in seeing His children suffer. He wants us to know that He will love us no matter what we do; we just have to repent and admit we were wrong—apologize to those we have wronged too, and that will be it."

"What? It's that easy?" She scowled.

He nodded.

"No way," she snapped, "that can't be true,"

Elias shrugged, "But I didn't say it," he circled his thumb on the bible on his lap, "this book right here says it. So, you better believe it and stop crying."

"Carla will *never* forgive me! Even James is angry."

"Yes, but that's today, what about tomorrow? What are you going to do about it? Sit here and refuse to come to church? Cook yourself to sleep?"

His last statement was meant as humor and she caught it well, smiling a little bit.

"There always will be these trying times when we fail the test; but it's what we do after that matters. Look, those two are one of the greatest couples I know. We need to keep them together; will you help me do that?"

She was a little hesitant now. For a moment, she had actually thought things would turn out differently after Carla had found out. James would take her in if Carla left, and they could get married out of town and... She realized how childish and incomplete her 'best' plan was. The church—and a lot of people would think she was a marriage wrecker of course... No wonder James had slammed her on the phone.

She looked up at the expectant man, "What can I do, pastor?"

"First, let's keep this on the low side; tell no one. You need to go and speak with Carla—apologize sincerely and tell her you never meant for it to happen."

She nodded dutifully, "I will, I will,"

"Tell me," he asked casually, "how long has this been going on?"

"Oh," her eyes widened, "we... it happened only today—this morning—I swear it—"

"It's ok—it's ok, take it easy," he raised both hands, "I was just asking, okay?"

"Okay," she nodded, breathing hard, "I'm so sorry... I was selfish and—I wanted him!"

Elias blinked, swallowing hard. She stared at him, feeling embarrassed but glad she had let her true feelings out.

"Go on..." he said calmly as if to encourage her.

"I have loved—no—liked him… for months now, since I came to the city. He's such a gentleman, handsome, rich and everything a girl could ask in a man. When he spoke to me about church and Jesus and all, I was moved, and I liked him even more. I guess… I liked him a little bit too much…"

"I guess you did," Elias smiled at her. He looked at his wristwatch and looked up, "You know, it's getting late, tomorrow is Sunday. Come to church tomorrow, and let's pray they both do. You and I will talk to them, yes?"

She still felt uneasy about approaching the fiery Carla Rosenberg but she knew it was a bitter pill she had to swallow.

She nodded in affirmation.

Five minutes later, as she saw the pastor drive away from her small yard, she wondered how she was going to face the woman whose husband she had slept with. She remembered the look on her face that morning when she had seen her. It was scary. The hatred in her eyes had chilled her. But she had to do it somehow… If God really had *already* forgiven her, then Carla eventually would. It was mission impossible.

Carla watched Josh sleeping peacefully in his cradle. She leaned forward and gently brushed a bunch of curly brown hair locks from his forehead. She felt a pain in her chest. They reminded her of her husband—her lying, cheating, egoistic husband. When had things gone so wrong?

"Honey?"

She turned around and saw Hannah in the doorway. She had a phone in her hand. *Her* phone.

"Someone called?" She wiped her face.

Hannah nodded, "It was Elias. Will you call him back?"

"He can't do anything to change my mind," Carla told her, "I want a divorce, and that's final."

"But you'll see him tomorrow, won't you?"

She blinked, "I'm not going to that church. I can stay home and pray. God is everywhere."

"Darling, you have to—"

"I don't have to do anything," she turned around, indicating the conversation was over. Hannah may have noticed, because she sighed and left.

Looking back down at her son, she was still perplexed. Was James aware he had a son when he was going to Petra's house? Did he think of the consequences? How could he?

She stroked the sleeping baby's face and he moved. She withdrew her hand quickly and took a step back. She longed to carry her son, as if it would give *her* some comfort. As she licked her lips and swallowed, it dawned on her. She was heartbroken. James had broken her heart. Her trust. It was over.

It was around 10 pm, and James found himself driving around the *Pop Top,* a part of the city he hardly frequented—and never at night. Filled with pubs, nightclubs, motels and casinos, it was the area he and Elias commonly referred to as *Sin City.* But he couldn't go home. It was Saturday night. He had been expecting Carla's return from her mother's in the next city... Well, he couldn't wait long enough, could he? A mistake led to another, and he ended up in bed with a girl he thought was like a mentee to him.

He made up his mind, and pulled up in front of a pub. The last time he frequented a pub was when he had still been in college, about nine years ago.

As he got out of his sedan, he looked down at his attire, as if to be sure he wasn't going to look out of place. In his white polo shirt and black denim pants, he looked a tad bit too well-dressed, contrary to the wild outfits worn by the pair of teenage girls who burst out of the pub at that moment. They looked drunk, holding on to each other and smiling sheepishly. They sauntered by him awkwardly, and he was little bit concerned for them. If they were going to drive, then it wasn't safe. Should he do something? Probably not. The last time he was trying to help a girl, he ended up in bed with her...

He walked casually to the open entrance and then with a sigh, walked into the pub. It was humid, noisy and reeked of alcohol. *Of course.* He realized people looked at him queerly as he weaved his way to the bar, avoiding looking at anyone. This was uncomfortable!

He was glad when he got to the bar, and was even happier when he saw the empty stools in front of the bar. The only other person seated was a skinny man at the extreme left, head down—minding his own drinking business.

The bartender, a heavyset man with balding blonde hair and a ring in one of the left handfingers appeared, unsmiling.

"What ya want, man?"

He sat on thestool right in front of the big man and cleared his throat, "Do you have any… soda?"

The man stuck a tongue in his cheek and scowled.

James shrugged, "Do you?"

"Listen, if you' a preacher or som'n like that, we don't do that here."

James was surprised, but he asked, "I'm not a preacher, please, but why don't you allow preachers in your bar? Aren't they citizens?"

"Well, they git shot or knifed, that's what they git," he folded his giant arms.

"Oh,"

"You gonna order or what?"

"I did. Soda."

"That's not alcohol," he quipped.

"I know," James nodded, "that's what I'll have."

The big man looked like he was going to say something, but another man stepped to James' right, clearing his throat. The big man instantly switched attention to him, his deep frown switching to a grin.

"Hey man," the bartender greeted, "this man here wan' trouble for 'imself here."

"Oh, he's just messing with you. He's my friend, James," the man's words made James turn to look at him. Meanwhile, the bartender started to chuckle, amused.

James didn't know how to react. It was Todd Mason, Carla's college sweetheart—the man who had kissed his *wife* in the mall. But James knew better. He knew Todd was staging a drama to probably save him, so he decided to play along.

"Hey Todd, you're late, as usual," he grinned.

"I am," Todd pulled back the stool to sit. He looked at the waiting bartender, "Give me the usual, and same here for my buddy James; he drinks like a champ."

"I thought so!" The bartender laughed, giving James a wink.

James just grinned foolishly at the big man until he turned the other way. Then he turned to the man beside him, his grin disappearing immediately.

"What do you want?"

"Oh, it's nice to meet you too, James," Todd smiled, "don't tell me you're still mad I kissed your wife by accident in the mall,"

"I'm not," he said quickly.

"Right..." he didn't believe him.

"Okay, so I'm mad so what? Why are you trying to interfere here?" James kept his voice lowered, "I don't drink and I am not going to start now. I'm also not here to chitchat with anyone, and not you!"

The bartender set two heavy mugs before them, causing James to turn around quickly. Before them were two full beer mugs. The bartender turned around after giving Todd a wave.

"See? It's just beer," Todd shrugged.

"Just beer?" James looked at him, "I'm not drinking."

"Suit yourself James," Before James could react, Todd picked the one before him and took a few deep gulps, before setting it down quickly.

Grabbing his own mug, he raised it in a toast, "Cheers..."

"You drink this much?" James just looked at him, shaking his head.

"So, how's the girl? How's Carla? Last I heard, she had a baby," Todd set down his glass after an initial gulp.

James remembered why he was there, and scowled, "Look, it's none of your business, and I'll appreciate it if you mind your own business."

Todd said nothing as James turned away. He felt his phone vibrate in his pocket, and he quickly rummaged through the right pocket of his denim pants. He looked at the screen and realized it was a message from Petra.

He saw Todd looking at him with a smile. He ignored him, and kept the phone to himself, opening the message to read:

> Hey, I wanted to say I'm sorry...
> I will apologize to Carla tomorrow after church.
> Really really sorry...

He sighed and shoved the phone back into his pocket. Why was she apologizing now? Earlier that afternoon, wasn't she the same person declaring her love for him?

He remembered Elias and understood. If anyone could make her change her mind like that, it was Elias. Thank God for Elias.

"So, I'm curious; what are you doing here at this time, James? Carla mad at you?" Todd asked casually.

James looked up at the other man and wondered why Carla could have dated him for three years. Yes, he looked a little handsome with his neatly cut black hair and muscular arms straining his tight black shirt, but that was probably it. Carla had told James Todd had opened his own garage in the city. James' job was as a manager in one of Blue Fin's largest banks.

Looking at Todd with glassy eyes, he ignored him and focused his hands on the bench before him.

"Look, it's okay to have trouble once in a while; we all have them, you know?" Todd said.

James realized he wasn't going to have any peace here. What had he been thinking? He got off the stool, and nodded at Todd, "See you around, Todd."

Todd remained surprisingly quiet as James started to walk away. James realized people still looked at him as he made his way out. He felt the fresh cool air hit his face when he stepped out. How were those people staying alive in that heat and smell? He walked to his car, using his key to unlock it. He spied a man at the entrance of the pub. He was big, and had an even bigger pair of blue jeans that looked like it was going to fall off him. His black jacket looked a bit too small, but the hood successfully shielded his face.

James wasn't comfortable, so he quickly entered his car and started it. Eyes on the man, he locked his doors, before reversing out of the small parking area in front of the pub.

As he headed home, he thought of one thing: Today was definitely the worst day of his life.

The chapel was a nice clean white building on the edge of an acre of a green field. It was a place that reminded Petra of a splendid wedding scene she had witnessed in one of her favourite movies.

Walking out of the church after the service had ended around 11 am, she was deeply disappointed neither James not Carla had come. At the moment, she was aware Pastor Elias was still busy answering questions inside, so she decided to walk out into the yard and wait till he was free.

She had barely stepped out when a hand closed on her shoulder, causing her to turn quickly. Her mouth went dry when she saw who it was. Hannah Madsen—Carla's mother. Of course, Carla would have told her about it. But wasn't she supposed to be in Barnesville?

With pleading eyes, she whispered, "Please, I am so sorry about—"

"Hush," Hannah quieted her, looking around, before looking back at her with an expressionless face, "Come with me."

She followed without a word, her heart beating faster. She followed the older woman to the large parking area behind the chapel, and stopped beside the old green Chevrolet that Hannah drove.

Hannah leaned against her car, hands akimbo, "Young woman, how are you?"

Nodding quickly, she answered, "I'm fine, madam,"

"Do you have any idea what you have done, child?" Hannah seemed to be trying hard not to lose her temper.

Petra knew that a few months ago, she would have walked away without a care, and probably start a new plan to seduce her man—that man had changed her life, and now it looked like she may have wrecked his...

"I am so sorry, I really am," she went on passionately, "I hoped she would come to church so that I can apologize in person. It wasn't James' fault. He's a good man and it was a mistake!"

Hannah didn't look surprised or impressed. She just sighed and blinked quickly. It looked like there was something on her mind, and she was struggling *not* to say it... Looking at her lean against the car, Petra felt sorry for her now.

"If there is anything I can do—I could go with you to see her now if you will allow me to."

Hannah smiled mirthlessly and shook her head. It was then that Petra saw that the old woman had been holding back tears. Seeing her eyes grow moist broke her heart. When an old woman grew teary in front of you, you had to feel it.

Without thinking, she rushed to hold her, but Hannah raised a hand to stop her. She blinked, and a large drop rolled down her right cheek.

Petra knew it was only a matter of time before the sorrow infected her too. As she stepped back and away from Hannah, she wiped her own eyes with her hands, and then rummaged in the purse and cried for a tissue. As she blew her nose, she heard someone else approaching. She looked around slowly and saw Pastor Elias only a few yards off, approaching them; his hands behind his back and a serious look on his face.

"What is going on here?" he looked from Petra to Hannah.

"It's nothing, Elias," Hannah told him, her voice croaky.

"Petra?" Elias looked to her for help.

"I don't know but I guess... it has to be about yesterday."

Elias looked at Hannah with a grave expression, "Auntie, you know there's more. What happened?"

Hannah cleared her throat and quickly cleaned her face with the back of her left hand.

"Yes?" Elias prodded.

"It's just that..." Hannah hesitated, "Carla isn't going to go back to him."

"Auntie, we can sort this out. It was only yesterday, so I can understand how she feels—"

"She left."

"What?!"

CHAPTER THREE

Carla sat near the window in the plane, looking down at the city beneath her. She looked away from the view and down at Josh. He was looking back at her with a lively smile, his left hand in his mouth. She lowered a hand and cleaned the drop of saliva that trickled down his chin.

"Hello, ma'am,"

She looked up and saw the pretty air hostess who had attended to her earlier.

"Is there a problem?" Carla looked at her expectantly.

"No," she smiled, "you have a beautiful baby," she told her.

Carla's smile was proud, "I do,"

"Do you need anything?" She asked pleasantly.

"Not at the moment, thank you," Carla smiled at her.

"Great," she waved and walked off, heels sounding on the floor as she left and went further ahead.

Carla sighed, leaning forward to plant a kiss on Josh's forehead. She had spoken to Larry, their lawyer, shortly before her departure. He had reluctantly agreed to meet James about the divorce. Meanwhile, she was headed for the Balearic Islands for some time to cool off. A holiday wasn't the worst thing in the world, she told herself.

"Besides, I need to meet new people," she said aloud to herself.

"Really?" A male voice startled her.

She had to reposition herself and turned almost 180 degrees to see the man sitting behind her. He looked fortyish, with receding black hair and lenses that reminded her of Harold Finch. He was a little smallish too, and was clad in a neat black suit and tie. He was smiling at her.

"Hi," he said simply in greeting with a wave of his left hand.

She caught sight of the ring on his finger, and somehow, it made her feel more at ease. She knew she was not ready for any sort of attention from men, and so a married man in a plane willing to keep his ring on definitely wasn't the kind to bother her.

"Hello," she forced a smile, "you were eavesdropping, don't you think, sir?"

"Sorry, I had to find a way of striking conversation," he said frankly, "I'm David; David Crossly."

"Carla," she nodded.

"I think you're going to have a stiff neck if you're going keep looking at me that way. Do you mind if I steal the seat next to you for a moment?"

She shrugged, "As long as you're paying for it,"

He chuckled and nodded, "Thank you,"

She watched as he got up noiselessly and then moved around to sit beside her. His eyes seem to have been drawn to Josh, and he was looking at the infant admiringly.

"My, Patricia was right," he grinned.

"Who's that, Mr. Crossly?" Carla looked amused.

"Oh, sorry, the air hostess,"

"Ah…" she nodded, "it's not your first time on this plane, is it?"

"It is," he smiled slyly, "I dated Patricia a few times."

"Oh," she was caught by surprise.

He laughed, "That was a joke,"

She laughed, "You got me there for a moment!"

"Do me a favour," he winked.

"That is?"

"Don't tell Patricia I said that,"

"I'll think about that!" She winked back.

"So," Crossly looked at Josh, "he doesn't have your blonde her or your pretty blue eyes… he looks like someone who's on this plane though…"

"Who?" She wondered what he was going to say this time.

"Come on," he grinned, "it has to be me,"

"No way!" She laughed, "Josh looks nothing like you!"

As she laughed out loud, she wasn't concerned about the handful of people in the VIP section of the plane. She had no idea she could laugh like this when she left Blue Fin. Somehow, a stranger had done it without so much as an effort.

"So," Crossly smiled gently, "where's the daddy?"

Her smile also grew thinner, and she shook her head gently.

"Oh, I'm terribly sorry... He must've been so young!" Crossly looked sad.

"No!" She interjected, "I didn't mean he was dead. He's... just not here."

"Oh," the twinkle retuned in his eyes, "so how are you heading to Mallorca without a man who looks like this?" he pointed down at Josh, "is he in a hospital bed?"

She smiled sadly, "No, but we're getting divorced,"

"Divorced?" Crossly said it with such venom that she felt she had said something bad. "Why?"

"Do I have to say?" She hoped she didn't sound rude.

He didn't seem offended at all. Instead, he adjusted himself in the seat and looked at her, "I know I'm a stranger, but let me make it easy for you. My name is Daniel David Crossly, and I am forty-eight years old. I have a wife who's twice my size, with twice the love I have for her, and she has given me three great children whom I love with all my heart... I am an accountant on the ground and a servant of the Lord in the air."

She looked at Crossly with renewed admiration, "That's really nice, Mr. Crossly; so you just get on any flight and what? Talk to people about the Lord?"

"I try my best," he told her, "are you a Christian, Carla?"

"Actually I am,"

"Very nice," he smiled, "then you know that the Great Commission in Matthew 28, specifically the verse 19 says 'Go ye therefore...'" he trailed off for her to add the rest.

"...and teach all nations, baptizing them in the name of the Father, and of the Son, and of the Holy Ghost."

"Fantastic," he gave her a little applause, "so I'm doing my part."

"But how can you constantly afford to sit in VIP and do this? There are a lot more people in economy you can preach to; they also need to hear, don't they?"

"Yes," he agreed, "but remember Mark 10: 25 dear, for it is easier for a camel to go through the eye of a needle than for a rich man to enter the kingdom of God."

She grinned, nodding, "You're a very clever accountant."

He laughed, "I guess I am."

"So I'm already a Christian, is there anything you want to tell me about, *pastor*?" She teased.

"Yes," he said pointedly, "your marriage."

She was suddenly alert. "What about it?"

"Don't end it, please..."

"What?"

"Yeah, I said it. Don't end your marriage to this child's father," he said more calmly, "not for the child's sake alone, but for yours, and for God's."

"Look, Mr. Crossly—"

"Call me David please,"

"David, I'm not happy saying this, but my husband cheated on me with a girl *he* brought to church, when I was returning home that day. I got home early, and realized he wasn't there. Our neighbour said she saw him leave in a hurry. I called Mel—our pastor's wife, and she said he wasn't with his best friend, the *pastor*. I accidently pass by the girl's street and I see his car! Guess what, I stopped and there he was, walking out of her door, tucking in his shirt! He didn't have to say it! But he did!"

"Listen," Crossly said calmly, "you must be really disappointed and hurt right now,"

"Actually yeah, I am!"

"And you should be,"

"Thank you!"

"But then what?"

"It's over,"

"Can I ask you a question, Carla?" Crossly leaned back in the seat, but kept his eyes on her.

"Sure,"

"What's the worst thing you have done in your life, Carla?"

"David, I like you and I respect you; I'll appreciate it if you respect my decision as well and not go ahead with this." She wasn't ready to go deeper. She was feeling enough hurt.

"I'm so sorry, if you would just answer this one, we won't go too far, Carla,"

She looked at him with a serious expression, "I had sex before marriage,"

He blinked, caught off-guard, but he cleared his throat quickly and went ahead, "Alright, but who do you think you offended in that case?"

She shrugged, "God of course,"

"Really?"

"Sure," she went on, "my body is God's temple, isn't it? I was supposed to save it for marriage. Look David, if you're going to say I offended my husband, it's not the same—I hadn't met him, wasn't a Christian and I thought I was going to marry the guy." She said defensively.

"I wasn't going to say that, no," Crossly shook his head, "I was going to ask how God took the offense. He might have been mad, right? Or?"

"I see where you're going with this. You want me to forgive him. Fine, I have, but he has to face the results of his actions. God endorses my divorce—"

"Does he?" Crossly arched a brow.

"Yes, he does," she went on, "God says explicitly that adultery is—"

"Ah, that one," Crossly smiled thinly, "what about the numerous others that say otherwise my dear? Matthew 19: 6... What God has put together, let no man—even you, put asunder. Paul added in 1 Corinthian 7: 10 that 'to the married I give this charge... not I, but the Lord: the wife should not separate from her husband'. "

Carla realized Crossly knew his bible and arguing with him was going to go nowhere. The hurt she felt wasn't going to go away, and she was beginning to get stressed by his views. She looked down and saw Josh sleeping.

"David, I think I'll like to rest now, if you please? I wouldn't want to wake him either," She motioned towards Josh, hoping the man would agree and just leave her alone.

He smiled and nodded, "Of course," he nodded, "just remember this; Jesus is waiting on you. He has prepared you all your life for this big test. Make him proud."

He got up quickly, and left her thinking. What was that supposed to mean? But as she sat there all alone, Crossly's last words seemed to ring in her ears again and again.

He has prepared you all your life for this big test

Make him proud

James was in bed when he heard his phone ringing. He rolled over to the table beside the bed, and took the phone to see the caller. He realized it was Elias. He was probably going to go on rattling on about why he didn't turn up in church.

He answered anyway, "Hello?"

"Still in bed?" Elias sounded casual, instead of harsh, as he expected.

"Yes,"

"Your wife is gone,"

"What do you mean gone?" He sat up quickly.

"Your lawyer will visit you tomorrow with divorce papers. Carla is off to the Balearic Islands. Are you going to go after her or you're going to stay and sign those papers?"

He was lost.

"Are you there, James?"

"I am,"

"What are you going to do?"

"I don't know Eli," James shook his head, "I don't know…"

"Should I come over?"

"No, I'll be fine. I'll call you back."

"Sure, stay safe, and keep praying, okay?"

"I will," James hung up and dropped the phone on the bed, staring up at the ceiling.

He couldn't believe it. A moment of pride, and his lovely wife was severing their ties—he wasn't sure if she had divorce in her mind before his unnecessary attack when she was leaving that Saturday afternoon. As he thought about it now, he realized his mistake.

"God," he murmured, "Save me."

CHAPTER FOUR

It was technically Hannah Madsen who saved the day—a week later. Well, to be fair, it was a little too late, because James had signed the papers after a scathing email from Carla about taking responsibility for one's actions. Elias had been devastated, and Petra equally shaken.

As for Hannah, she had a heart attack, and that brought Carla's Spanish holiday adventure to a premature end. She arrived the following day, and rushed to Hannah's side at the hospital. She was going to be fine, the doctors said.

Carla was aware her imminent break up with her husband was a factor in her mother's demise, and it infuriated her the more. Not only was James' actions affecting her, it was now affecting her mother as well! Three days after arriving back at Blue Fin, she was ready to take her mother back home. She knew James would have been there, but that was why she had texted him not to step foot in the hospital...

James was reading his bible, sitting at his desk inside his den. When he saw his phone rang, he rolled his eyes. He wasn't in the mood for picking phone calls. He didn't want any criticism from the church folk who had heard about the divorce.

He reluctantly took his phone and realized it was Petra. He cut the line and put the phone back on the table. He didn't need anything from her. He was to blame for everything, she didn't have to try so hard to share the blame.

He was reading again when the phone rang once more. Annoyed, he took it and set it on silent mode. Satisfied, he sat back and continued his reading.

Three hours later, when he was dozing, he decided he needed to go to bed. He got up, stretching and yawning loudly. He glanced at his phone and was astonished to see it was ringing *again*. What was going on with Petra?

He took the phone and answered, "What is wrong with you?!"

"James!" She sounded relieved and agitated at the same time, "Thank God!"

"What is it? It's almost 11 pm."

"Your wife—sorry, I mean Carla—she was in an accident!"

"Oh my God," was all James could say.

"James, where have you been? I've been—"

"I know-I know!" He quipped, suddenly alive, "where is she? Where is she now?!"

"She's at the John Harper Hospital. She's had surgery, but she's under sedation now," she informed him.

"I'm coming over right now!" He was already rushing out of the den, his free hand searching his pockets for his car keys.

"I don't know if you'll be able to see her at—"

"I don't care!" He cut the connection, dashing out his front door after discovering his keys in his back pocket.

He jumped into his black sedan and screeched away.

When James arrived at the hospital, the atmosphere was calm. Hannah had not been told, because she was also still hospitalized. Elias and his wife Melanie were there with Petra, who kept blaming herself for everything.

When the doctor came to meet the four of them in the corridor, James stepped up to him quickly.

"When can I see her, doc?"

"That would have to be tomorrow, I'm afraid sir," he sounded apologetic, "she needs her rest now."

"But could you give some more detail? "

"She lost a lot of blood, she had really bad cuts in her side; but the surgery was successful," he explained, "We have to watch carefully and hope she stabilizes tomorrow."

James did not have the courage to ask the difficult questions—he saw the look on the doctor's face and could tell he was nervous. He didn't ask about her chances because he didn't want to know. Once she's *supposed to* stabilize, that had to be good. Whatever reason that was causing the young doctor to sweat, he hoped it wasn't serious.

James joined the pastor and his wife on the bench a little way off, avoiding looking at Petra who stood farther away.

"James," Melanie's small voice got his attention.

"Yes?" He realized his voice was hoarse.

"Why don't you go talk to that girl? She's blaming herself, and it's a matter of time before she breaks down, you know?"

Melanie was the quiet kind, so whenever she spoke, she probably meant it. James looked to Elias, who just looked back without a word.

"She shouldn't blame herself. This is on *me*," James said, "you should let her know that."

"She looks up to you, whether or not you two did the wrong thing," Melanie told him, "please, just look at her…"

James turned to see Petra leaning against the wall, looking like she was going to fall and die. Her usual glowing face was unbelievably pale, and she looked like she had lost some weight too.

James turned to Melanie, nodded and got up.

He walked towards Petra. She saw him coming, and straightened. She looked cautious.

"Is there anything you want me to do?" She asked quickly.

"Yes," James dropped an arm on her shoulder and felt her stiffen, "stop blaming yourself for everything. We have two women in hospital beds; we don't want to add another." He forced a smile.

She forced a smile back, "I won't be in a hospital bed."

"We all have to move on," he told her, "we make mistakes, but we are alive and we have the chance to correct them. As long as we live, there's hope in Christ."

"You sound like my teacher again," she heaved a relieved sigh.

He lifted his hand from her shoulder, "You know, I can't wait for her to wake up. I want to just kneel before her and apologize for all I've done to her."

"Do you think she'll take you back?" Petra sounded positive, "That would be so, so great."

"I hope she will, but that's not why I'm going to do it…"

"Why?"

"I want her to forgive me," he explained, "until she does, nothing else can happen. If she does, and decides she doesn't want me back, I will accept that. Now that adversity is evident, I see my flaws so clearly,"

"Flaws? Do *you* have flaws?" She wondered.

"I do!" James nodded quickly, "I'm selfish, proud, a bully, I judge people—"

"Then I must be a very bad person," she smiled broadly, the colour coming back to her face.

"It's good to see you smile again," he told her, "now, stop dwelling on what has happened and look to—"

The loud beeping sound made James stop in mid-sentence, eyes darting in the direction of Elias and Melanie. They were on their feet. Nurses were rushing past him suddenly, and he saw the young doctor accompanying an older one into the room Carla was being held. Exchanging a quick look with Petra, they dashed towards them.

They all stood plastered to the door, waiting anxiously for anyone to come out. It wasn't long before the older doctor came out, a frown on his wrinkled face.

"Doc, what's wrong?" James was fastest to ask.

"I'm sorry" he looked up with a grim look, everyone's breath was held, "she's going to need a kidney."

James had wandered out of the John Harper Clinic—to clear his head. If he didn't know better, he would have believed God was punishing him. In just one week, his life had turned upside down... When he had heard the news, he knew it was over. It wasn't the divorce anymore, it was death that was looming...

As he took a turn into the dark alley behind the hospital's walls he realized he had not been in this part of the city since his High School days. His mother would warn him about thugs—she had been a midwife at John Harper right until her death after her cancer ten years ago.

As he walked through the alley, it reeked of rotting fish. He thought he heard footsteps behind him, and sharply turned around. His eyes widened in horror. It may have been a little dark, but he recognized the hooded man he had seen in front of the pub a week ago.

"Hey, what do you want? I've got no change but you can have—" He was putting his hands in his back pockets to find his wallet.

"Go to hell, preacher boy," he growled.

"I'm not—" he gasped when he saw the unmistakable blade sticking out of the man's right hand.

"You were saying?" he grinned, "are you not going to scream?"

He gulped. What a night, he thought. The night the Rosenberg family tree ended. Running crossed his mind. The man was big, so he could outrun him.

He looked at the long blade and guessed it was about five inches long. He wasn't ready to die. Making up his mind, he counted silently in his head, about to make a run for it.

He was caught by surprise when the man leaped forward just before he could take off, pinning him to the cold dirty wall of the alley.

"Please," he gasped, "don't kill me; don't kill me!"

"I love it when I see preacher boys like you begging for it!" He showed James the full length of his knife, the blade gleaming lightly in the semi-darkness.

"Yes, I'm begging you, sir, please let me go, and God will reward you!"

"God?" He spat, "That was the wrong answer,"

Before James could react, he jammed the knife into him...

Three days later...

Carla's eyes fluttered open, and she was marvelled at the people who smiled at her, clapping happily. Her mother was there, smiling back at her. Josh was in her arms. Elias and Melanie were there as well. She was surprised to see Todd! He winked at her, and she shook her head a little bit. Her smile waned when she saw Petra looking back at her with a genuine smile. Well, it looked like James was not man enough to be there after all. Not that she hated him anymore—in her time of pain and suffering, she had been granted the peace to gather her thoughts and reflect on her life. She had been awake for hours, but had spent her time reflecting... She had realized she was as imperfect as her proud husband—ex-husband.

James may have been proud, but he was a willing evangelist, and a great teacher... He was kind and very generous... He was romantic, and she loved that about him. Despite her self-assured nature, she had realized she had been staring at her strong-headed and impulsive unforgiving self the past week. She wished she could turn back the clock... It had been *her* decision to leave home and spend a month with her mum—after watching James endure twelve months in the same house without his wife…

Her breath caught in her throat when she saw David Crossly! He was sitting behind Petra. He winked at her.

"So," Elias got up, "you're finally awake, and Mr. Crossly here wanted to say something to you as soon as you wake up."

"You know, Matthew 19: 8 does—" Crossly started as soon as he got on his feet.

She cleared her throat, "Before you say anything," she was surprised at how hoarse she sounded, "I need to say this…"

"Go ahead," Crossly was smiling.

"I *do* remember 1 Corinthians 13 you know? Love is kind, doesn't envy or boast, it is not arrogant or rude; neither does it insist on its own way," she breathed hard, but raised her hand when Elias was about to stop her, "the last part is like… hopes all things, *endureth*all things…" She smiled at Petra, who was surprised but smiled back, and then she looked to Crossly gratefully, "I was wrong."

Crossly and Elias exchanged congratulatory looks.

"So, where is James?" She asked no one in particular, "He's not here, and I'm going to beat him for it, but can someone call him?"

She realized everyone remained uncomfortably quiet. She looked to Elias for an explanation; she knew something was wrong.

"Umm, after your accident, you needed a kidney, so—"

"I needed a *what*?" She was astonished, and despite her condition, she was forcing herself to sit. Petra rushed to her side, helping her. She knew Carla wasn't going to lie still.

"He was attacked in an alley and stabbed to the point of death," Elias said.

"Oh my God..." She put a shaking hand to her chest, tears welling up in her eyes in volumes.

"He instructed his kidney be given to you—you know you guys have a lot in common... blood type..."

"I know," she whispered, "I know… I love him, and I'm so sorry… So sorry… Oh dear God…"

As she burst into tears, everyone was looking up at Elias still.

"Carla, he's alive and he's in the next room. What are you going to do?"

"What?" She looked from Petra to everyone else. They were beaming at her, Hannah and Melanie wiping away their tears. Turning to Petra, she asked, "Can we go there now?"

Petra nodded quickly, "He's resting, but he'll be excited to see you."

"Of course he will be," she said aloud, "I'm his wife!"

A week later, James Rosenberg was discharged and he was reunited with his *wife* at home, with their son, Joshua. They had not only planned a remarriage, but they planned a grand wedding in fact… And so a month later, Petra watched as her favourite movie scene played before her very eyes—seeing a wedding happen in the white church set amidst the green grassy field. Everyone knew they were meant to be by the sheer wonderment of their survival.

While James walked hand in hand with his bride after the ceremony, Carla spotted Petra standing with Crossly and the air hostess, Patricia! She pulled James along to meet them.Petra hugged them both, first Carla, and then the ever-smiling James.

"Carla," Crossly grinned, "Meet my daughter and colleague in the gospel, Patricia Crossly,"

"Are you serious?!" Carla laughed, but James and Petra just looked on, confused.

Crossly and Patricia joined in the laughter, very much aware of the prank Crossly had played on her back in the plane to the Balearic Islands.

Carla turned to James, "Can you believe these two ambushed me in a plane?"

"Really?" James feigned a look of surprise, "they look harmless to me,"

"But seriously," Carla grinned at Patricia, ", and no offense David, but you look nothing like him. You're stunning!"

Crossly and James laughed, while Patricia giggled, "Thank you, Carla,"

"Where's my maid of honour, Petra?" Carla looked around. She wasn't there.

James spotted her ahead and smiled, "Ah, there she is!"

Carla followed her husband's finger and was delighted at what she saw. A handsome young man was talking animatedly to her, and Petra looked on with a smile, nodding on with interest. She laughed at something he said and he looked even happier.

"That's a great picture, she doesn't like any of the boys at church," Carla smiled.

"She likes me," James joked.

"Yep," Carla nodded, "so does every girl in the church, Prince Charming,"

"Oh look who's coming!" Crossly signalled to them.

They looked around and saw a smiling Hannah carrying Josh.

"Aww, my baby...!" Carla grabbed him and gave him a kiss on the lips.

James cleared his throat. Carla turned to James and planted a kiss on his lips too, "Don't worry, I love you too..."

CONCLUSION

Summary

The story of James and Carla Rosenberg tells a tale of unfaithfulness and how a Christian family battled the common phenomenon with their religious background, individual characters, and personal sentiments.

James cheated on his wife with Petra Gonzalez, but after his wife found out, he was faced with divorce. His best friend Pastor Elias Potter spoke to him and then Petra, successfully convincing Petra to repent and seek to help mend the broken marriage. However, James' pride held him back.

With divorce pending, Carla left the country on a holiday to clear her mind, but is forced to return due to her mother's heart attack. She was involved in a fatal accident and needed a kidney to live. That night, her now-repentant ex-husband was nearly stabbed to death , but provided her his kidney to save her life. However, hernear death experience prompted to reflect on her life and change her mind about the divorce. They remarried after they both had made full recoveries...

Lesson

The need for forgiveness no matter how hard is underlined by Carla's reflection on the true meaning of love as described by Paul in 1 Corinthians 13:4-13. In our imperfect world, sin and offense abound and our ability to radiate Christ's love and mercy plays a key role in achieving happiness in our relationships. Knowing one's boundaries as a single/ married Christian also reflects in the story—Pride, as depicted initially by James is manifested as a negative trait in relationship.